Other Flossie Crums titles:

Flossie Crums and The Fairies Cupcake Ball
Flossie Crums and The Enchanted Cookie Tree

Flossie Crums

and the
Royal Spotty
Dotty Cake

By Helen Nathan
Illustrated by Daryl Stevenson

PAVILION
CHILDREN'S

To Molly, Rosie, Lottie and Larry xx with love. HN
For Tim, Ben and Miranda with love. DS xxx

This edition first published in the United Kingdom in 2011 by
Pavilion Children's Books
10 Southcombe Street
London W14 0RA
An imprint of Anova Books Company Ltd

Text copyright: Helen Nathan 2011
Illustrations: Daryl Stevenson 2011
Photographs: Anova Books 2011

Photographer: Noel Murphy
Home economist: Karen Taylor
Stylist: Sarah O'Keefe
Book design: Lee-May Lim

10 9 8 7 6 5 4 3 2 1

ISBN 9781843651888
Printed by 1010 Printing International Ltd, China

This book can be ordered direct from the publisher at the website: www.anovabooks.com

Have you
ever wondered if
fairies eat cake? Well, let me
tell you, **THEY LOVE CAKE** and
so do I – do you too?

Hiding on every page, is a tiny fairy – *see if you can spot*
one! Sometimes you might have to look really hard to find
them. Grown ups will often miss them, *so*
you might have to help.

Hello! I'm Flossie Crums, aged seven and three quarters. I'm just an ordinary girl, but I also happen to be the Royal Baker of the Fairy Kingdom of Romolonia! Ever since, I was little I've always made special cakes, but now I bake for the fairies too.

My Cookery Book

by Flossie Crums

I keep all my recipes in this little book.

My Mum

My Dad

My dog Rocket

My Family

...and my fairy friends

My Cat Goliath

My little brother Billie. He likes collecting bugs..., yuck!

"When are they going to get here?"
asked Billie, for about the millionth time.

"At half-past Bluebell!"
I said crossly.

"Whenever that is!"

The royal family had invited us to visit them. But first, the fairies had to come and 'mini-mize' us so we would be small enough to enter through the tiny door in our chestnut tree into the Magical Kingdom of Romolonia.

At last, a small door magically appeared in the trunk.
It creaked open and Plum and Cherry flitted out.

"Sorry we're late, but Honey got her head stuck
in a watering-can," explained Cherry.

"We had to butter her head just to get it out!"

Billie and I giggled,
Honey was always doing silly things.

"Are you ready?" asked Plum.

"Ready!" we replied.

Billie held my hand tightly as Plum flew around
and around us in a shower of tiny stars.
We grew smaller and smaller until we
were tiny enough to fit through the door.

The door closed with a 'BANG' behind us.

We
followed
the fairies
down the corridor of
golden apple trees,
past the door of the Lollipop Ballroom
and the tall frosty spires
of the Ice Cream Palace.

Then round the next corner
Plum and Cherry
stopped in front of
a pink and
white door which was made
of something soft and squishy.

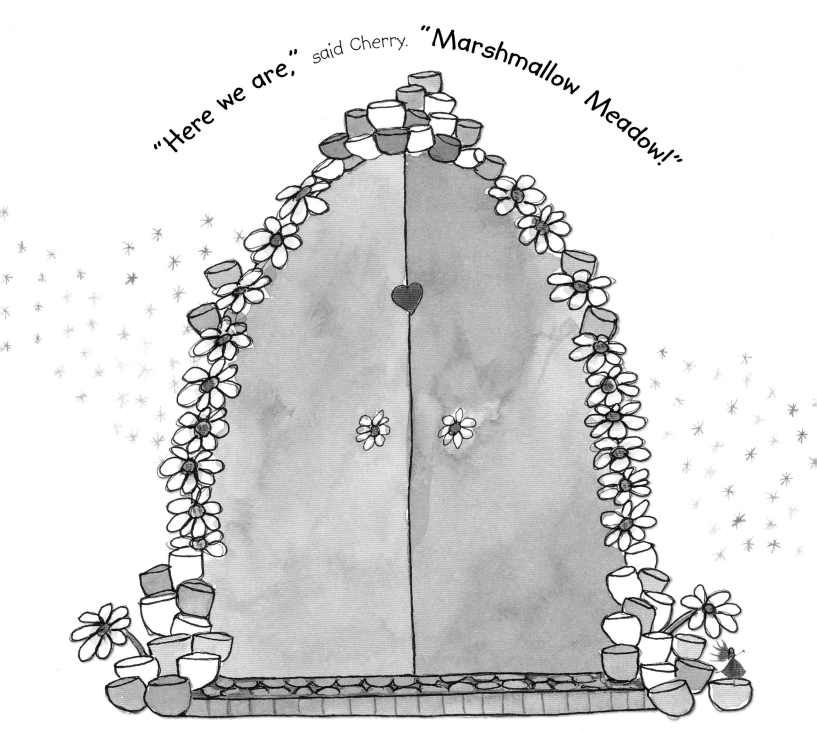

"Here we are," said Cherry. "Marshmallow Meadow!"

She pushed open the door and we gasped.

There were **rainbow** coloured sheep and
tiny green rabbits grazing in a meadow of
marshmallow daisies.

King Saffron was standing under a purple pear tree, looking very grand and important. His wife, Queen Rosie, sat cradling Princess Cornflower. Her Majesty's fairies-in-waiting Crystal and Plum were in attendance and little Minty and Honey fidgeted at her feet.

"Ah," said Queen Rosie.

"Flossie Crums Royal Baker of Romolonia and Billie the Brave... Welcome!"

"Your Majesty," I said, remembering to curtsey while Billie did a really good bow.

Princess Cornflower's apple-blossom-pink cheeks glowed and her cornflower-blue eyes sparkled. She made the cutest little gurgling and cooing noises... then suddenly she burped!

"Hey!" said Billie laughing. **"When I do that everyone tells me off!"**

We took turns holding the baby,
until it was time for the fairies to change
her nappy...

poo... yuck!

We weren't hanging
around for that!

Instead of nappy changing, Crystal showed us how to tell **flower-time.**

(Flower-time is just like human-time except there are flowers instead of numbers.)

Then suddenly it was pansy o'clock (that's five o'clock, see!) and it was time to go home.

"Come on Billie we've got to go.

I want to make a cake for the baking competition in the village fair."

"You're bound to win!" said Cherry kindly. **"Your cakes are the best in your world – and in ours!"**

But I wasn't so sure. An old lady called Miss Batty had won first prize for the last three years running.

We waved goodbye to everyone. Plum led us back to the doorway to our garden. As she spun round and round us, flying in the opposite direction, Billie and I grew bigger and bigger until we were back to our normal size.

"Bye bye," she waved and disappeared back through the door which then magically melted away.

I plonked myself down at the kitchen table to design my cake. I was just taking out my orange and yellow pencils when I heard a loud scream.

"Aaaaagggggghhh!" Billie yelled, running into the kitchen with a box in his hand.

"One of my worms has escaped."

He put the box on the table and the others started crawling out as well. (Honestly, how was I supposed to work with giant worms creeping around all over the place?)

"I can't find it anywhere," he said. "Help me find it Floss."

"No way! Go away, I'm busy."

(Does anyone want to buy an almost-new 6 year-old brother?)

I decided my entry in the cake competition would be a brilliant double-decker Orange and Lemon Spotty Dotty Cake.

Billie then disappeared into the garden with Rocket and his horrid box of worms and I was finally left alone to bake in peace – phew!

I was busy mixing when Honey flew in.

"Can I watch as you bake, please?"

asked Honey sweetly.

"Yes, of course you can. Would you like a tiny taste?"

She was just reaching forward for a lick when the door suddenly flew open and Billie and Rocket came charging into the kitchen.

"Look what we've found!" said Billie excitedly.

Curled up on his **very** dirty hand was an **enormous** hairy caterpillar. "Isn't it beautiful?"

"No Billie, it's not beautiful take it..."

"Wooff!"

Rocket had spotted Honey!

"AAAAgggrrrhhhhh!"

screamed Honey, toppling off the edge of the bowl and falling head first into the cake mix!

"Bluummmfff," wailed poor Honey.

"Blmmmfff, mmmerbbble, bbbllerbble, blmmmmfff!"

"I'll get her out," said Billie as he plunged his filthy hands into the cake mix.

Billie lifted out a wriggling, squiggling lump from the mixture and put Honey gently back on the table.

I was staring sadly at my muddy cake mix, when Crystal and Plum appeared. They looked **very** glum.

"What's wrong?"
I asked.

"It's King Saffron," sniffed Plum. "He's very sick and nobody knows what's the matter with him."

"Queen Rosie made him special honeysuckle tea," whispered Crystal. "And we're all taking turns to fan him with marigold leaves but nothing seems to help."

"We know that laughter is the best medicine," said Plum.

"But we can't even make him smile."

"The Queen has sent us to get Honey," said Plum, looking around the kitchen.

"Do you know where she is?"

"Here I am," said a small voice from behind the mixing bowl.

"What happened to you?!" asked Crystal.

"Never mind about that now," said Plum briskly. "We have to get back."

The three fairies rushed away to get back to the King and Queen.

I turned back to my ruined cake mix, scraped the whole lot into the bin and started again.

When the cake was finally finished, I fetched the star wand that Queen Rosie gave me the first time I went to Romolonia and waved it over the icing.

Sparkles exploded in the air, leaving a dusting of fairy glitter.

Orange and Lemon Spotty Dotty Cake

What you need:

Cake
175g/6oz/¾ cup softened butter
175g/6oz/¾ cup caster sugar
175g/6oz/1½ cups self-raising flour
3 medium eggs, beaten
1 tsp baking powder
grated rind and juice of 1 large orange

Icing
juice of 1 large orange
200g/7oz/1½ cups icing sugar

For special occasions you can also use:
One packet each of ready-to-roll orange and lemon icing, orange food-safe glitter,
a set of round baby biscuit cutters and orange spotty ribbon.

What you do:
Preheat the oven to 180°C/350°F/gas mark 4. Use a little extra butter to grease a 20.5cm/8 inch round cake tin. Get help to line the tin with greaseproof paper.

Put all the cake ingredients in a bowl and beat well with a wooden spoon until everything is mixed together and there are no lumpy bits.

Spoon all the mixture into the tin, get help to put it in the oven, then bake for 35 minutes. Ask a grown-up to test if the cake is cooked by inserting a skewer in the middle – it should come out clean. If it doesn't, cook a little longer

Get help to take the cake out of the oven. Leave it in the tin for a few minutes, then turn it out of the tin onto a wire rack and leave to cool.

When the cake has completely cooled, make the icing in a seperate bowl by mixing the squeezed orange juice with the icing sugar. Use a blunt knife to spread the icing onto the cake. Then, for top competitions, roll out ready-to-roll icing and drape it over the cake (the orange icing acts as glue). Trim it to the shape of the cake. Make spots in a different colour from ready-to-roll icing. Before you stick on the spots, cover them in edible glitter, then stick them on all over the cake.

(I doubled the cake and icing quantities to make a two-tiered cake, but I used a 23cm/9 inch and a 15cm/6 inch tin to make it look special, like a wedding cake. I stacked the small one on top and 'glued' it with icing then decorated with ribbon round the edge of both cakes.)

I am very
proud of
this cake!

**ORANGE AND LEMON
SPOTTY DOTTY**

CAKE !

Billie's head appeared around the door.

"Floss, I've had a brainwave for the baking competition! It's genius. I'm going to make a pile of chocolate brownies covered with **jelly worms** and loads of indoor **sparklers**.

I'm going to call them my 'Exploding Toffee and Chocolate Brownies' – it's going to be brilliant!"

Mum, who'd just walked in, chuckled.

"OK Billie, we'll bake together. I'm going to enter with Granny Torcallini's famous White Chocolate Ring-a-Ring-a-Roses Cake. She taught me how to make it years ago. You've got the recipe in your book, haven't you Flossie?"

Granny Torcallini's
White Chocolate Ring-a-Ring-a-Roses Cake

What you need:

Cake	Icing
125g/4oz/½ cup butter	115g/3¾ oz/just under ½ cup soft unsalted butter
190g/6½oz/1¾ cups self-raising flour	
100g/3½oz white chocolate	175g/6oz white chocolate, melted and cooled slightly
2 medium eggs, whisked	
200g/7oz/just under 1 cup caster sugar	115g/3¾ oz/just under 1 cup icing sugar
1 tsp vanilla essence	1 tsp pure vanilla extract
125ml/4fl oz/½ cup milk	5 white chocolate roses or white chocolate truffles

What you do:

Preheat the oven to 180°C/350°F/gas mark 4. Use a little extra butter to grease a 20.5cm/8 inch round cake tin. Get help to line the tin with greaseproof paper.

Put the butter, white chocolate, caster sugar and millk in a pan and heat until melted. Cool for 10 minutes, then stir in the flour, eggs and vanilla.

Spoon all the mixture into the tin, get help to put it in the oven, then bake for 25 minutes. Ask a grown-up to test if the cake is cooked by inserting a skewer in the middle – it should come out clean. If it doesn't, cook a little longer.

Get help to take the cake out of the oven. Leave it in the tin for a few minutes, then turn it out of the tin onto a wire rack and leave to cool completely.

To make the icing, put the butter in a bowl and use a handheld electric mixer to beat it until creamy. Beat in the melted white chocolate.

Add the icing sugar and vanilla and beat at low speed, scraping the sides and bottom of the bowl, until light and fluffy (this takes about 10 minutes).

Cover the cake with the white chocolate icing and decorate with white chocolate roses (or white chocolate truffles look good too).

WHITE CHOCOLATE RING-A-RING-A-ROSES

CAKE

It looks great with white chocolates too!

BILLIE'S
EXPLODING TOFFEE AND CHOCOLATE BROWNIES WITH JELLY WORMS!

These are
Really yummy!

Billie's Exploding Toffee and Chocolate Brownies with Jelly Worms!

What you need:
160g/5½oz/¾ cup softened butter
160g/5½oz dark chocolate
3 medium eggs
250g/9oz/just over 1 cup caster sugar
50g/2oz chocolate toffees, cut into small chunks
110g/3¾oz/1 cup plain flour
jelly worms, indoor sparklers

What you do:
Preheat the oven to 180°C/350°F/gas mark 4. Using a little extra butter, grease a 20.5cm/8inch square tin (or, even better, use a silicone brownie tin).

Put the butter and dark chocolate in a saucepan on the hob and leave over a gentle heat until melted. Stir together, then take off the heat and leave to cool for 5 minutes.

Using a wooden spoon, mix the eggs with the sugar and add to the melted chocolate. Add the chocolate toffee chunks and flour, then mix everything together.

Spoon all the mixture into the tin and get help to put it in the oven, then bake for 25 minutes.

Get a grown-up to help take the tin out of the oven, then let it cool. Cut into 12 brownie squares.

Pile up on a plate and serve with jelly worms and indoor sparklers!

I was busy putting the cakes into the cake boxes, ready for the fair later that afternoon, when Candy flew in looking very upset.

"Oh Flossie we don't know what to do! King Saffron is getting worse. He's covered in HUGE spots from head to toe. Look, at this picture of him. He's so miserable that even funny little Honey can't make him smile. Can you think of anything to cheer him up?"

As she was talking, she glanced down... and realising she was standing on my cake, she began to giggle.

"What's so funny, Candy?" I asked.

"Oh Flossie! It's wonderful. It's the most wonderful cake I've ever seen!

And with the spots... the spots... Flossie... your cake... looks just like King Saffron!"

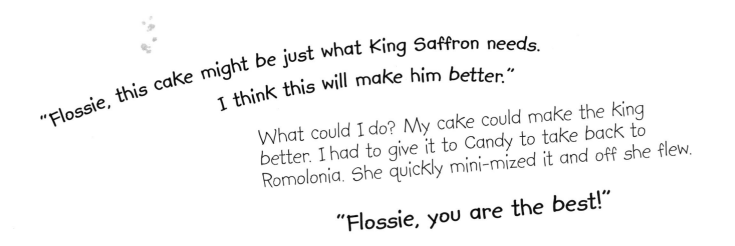

"Flossie, this cake might be just what King Saffron needs. I think this will make him better."

What could I do? My cake could make the King better. I had to give it to Candy to take back to Romolonia. She quickly mini-mized it and off she flew.

"Flossie, you are the best!"

"Where's your cake Floss?" said Billie as he came into the kitchen with mum.

"I gave it to Candy to take to poor old spotty King Saffron."

"Oh Flossie," said Mum. "What a sweet and generous thing to do. You are a very kind girl."

"Thanks mum, it was the right thing to do. Come on let's get going, the fair's already started. Someone's got to beat Miss Batty this year!"

The fair was brilliant. Dad bought us balloons and candyfloss.

Bertie Sugarman, the rather large, jolly Mayor of Little Lickington, announced on the loud speaker that he was about to judge the cake competition.

"He'll be a good judge," whispered Billie.

"He looks like he's eaten a lot of cakes."

"Ah," said Mayor Sugarman, beaming at the cakes.
"My favourite part of the fair."

"But Billie," I whispered quietly. "Where are your brownies?"

"Ummm.... Olly and me and Freddie Witherspoon ate them," he said. "We didn't mean to, we just ate a little worm each and then we couldn't stop."

Mayor Sugarman looked at the empty plate.

"**Oh**," he chuckled. "**Looks like someone beat me to it... not much to judge here!**"

Next he tasted Mrs Blynkington-Smythe's Crunchy Lemon and Honey Drizzle Cake. "**Very lemony,**" he said, putting the rest of the slice back on the plate.

Then it was the turn of Miss Batty's cake. He took a small minty bite, then he took a big chocolatey bite and then he finished the whole piece.

Oh no! He definitely liked it.

Billie Crums

Mrs Blynkington-Smythe

Flossie Crums

Finally it was time for Mum's cake.

The Mayor looked admiringly at the beautiful Ring-a-Ring-a-Roses cake, picked up a slice and took a dainty bite and licked his lips.

He closed his eyes and went "Mmmmmmm... mmmmmmmm."

People giggled and Mum's face was starting to turn pink when he suddenly opened his eyes.

"First Prize," he declared. "Absolutely delicious!"

Mum then blurted out, "Thank you, but it is my daughter Flossie, who is the real baker in the family. If she hadn't very kindly given away her cake to a friend who's not well, I'm sure it would have won first prize!'"

I nudged Billie, "You might have won if you hadn't scoffed the lot!"

Mrs Crums

Miss Batty

I was smiling at mum when suddenly....

"Psst! Flossie! Down here!"

I peered into a bunch of yellow and orange marigolds –
and there was Minty among the flowers.

"Minty," I whispered. "What are you doing here? Someone might see you!"

"I doh," said Minty. "But I had to tell you... King Saffron is feeling buch, buch better and it's all because of your cake...

BBWWAAAACHHHOOO!!!!"

It was a very big sneeze for a very little fairy and everyone looked around to see where it had come from, so I quickly rubbed my nose.

"I think I bight be allergic to barrigolds,"
said Minty, sniffing.

"Oh, I'm so glad he's better. Thank you for coming to tell me. But you must go, before someone sees you."

"Ok," said Minty. She flew out of the marigolds and off into the dusk. "Dighty-dight Flossie!"

I woke up the next morning feeling a little bit sad.
The cake competition was over and I'd have to wait
364 days until the next one.

But suddenly the fairies
fluttered in – and this time
they had a royal visitor with
them! Princess Cornflower!

In her tiny hands, she had a long necklace made from cornflowers.

"Goo goo, ga, bla"

"What I think the princess is trying to say," giggled Honey. "Is thank you for making her Daddy better."

Princess Cornflower fluttered over my head and placed the garland of flowers around my neck. Then she planted a tiny kiss on my cheek and did a little burp!

Flowers from a princess and a happy King. I love being the Royal Baker of Romolonia.

THE END...

...Well, not quite.

I thought you might like to have the other cake recipes from the Village Fair. Mrs Blinkington-Smythe has very kindly given me her special recipe for Crunchy Lemon and Honey Drizzle Loaf.

MRS. BLYNKINGTON-SMYTHE'S

CRUNCHY LEMON AND HONEY DRIZZLE CAKE

Mrs Blynkington-Smythe's
Crunchy Lemon and Honey Drizzle Cake

What you need:
Cake
100g/3½oz/½ cup softened butter
175g/6oz/¾ cup caster sugar
175g/6oz/1½ cups self-raising flour
1 tsp baking powder
grated rind of 1 lemon
4 tbsp milk
2 medium eggs

Crunchy Lemon and Honey Drizzle Icing
juice of 1 lemon
100g/3½oz/½ cup caster sugar
1 tsp runny honey

What you do:
Preheat the oven to 180°C/350°F gas mark 4. Use a little extra butter to grease a 25.5cm/10 inch loaf tin.

Put all the cake ingredients into a large bowl and mix together with a wooden spoon for about 2 minutes.

Spoon all the mixture into the tin, get a grown-up to help put it in the oven, then bake for 35 minutes.

While the cake is cooking, make the icing – squeeze the lemon and mix the juice with the caster sugar and honey.

As soon as the cake comes out the oven (ask someone to help you), very carefully drizzle the lemony honey sugar over the cake while it is still in the tin. This must be done slowly, allowing the lemon juice to sink into the cake. Leave the cake to cool.

When the cake has cooled, carefully lift out of the tin and eat!

I had to really beg Miss Batty for her Chocolate and Mint Marble cake, but she finally let me write it into my recipe book:

MISS BATTY'S
CHOCOLATE AND MINT MARBLE CAKE

I love this green colour it's so cool!

Miss Batty's
Chocolate and Mint Marble Cake

What you need:
225g/8oz/1 cup softened butter
225g/8oz/1 cup caster sugar
225g/8oz/2 cups self-raising flour
4 medium eggs, beaten
1 tsp baking powder
1 tbsp cocoa powder
2 tbsp hot water
½ tsp mint essence
1 tsp green food colouring (if you like)
icing sugar to sprinkle

What you do:
Preheat the oven to 180°C/350°F/gas mark 4. Use a little extra butter to grease a 23cm/9 inch ring mould.

Mix the first five ingredients together in a bowl with a wooden spoon until well blended.

Sift the cocoa powder into another bowl and add the hot water. Divide the cake mixture evenly between 2 bowls. Add the cocoa to the mixture in one bowl, and add the the mint essence and food colouring to the other bowl. You will now have one chocolate cake mix and one minty green cake mix!

Spoon alternate blobs of each cake mixture next to each other into the tin until all of the mint and chocolate mixture is in the mould.

Get help to put it in the oven and bake for 40 minutes. Ask a grown-up to help take the tin out of the oven and leave until cool.

When the cake is cool, tip out of the tin and sprinkle with icing sugar.

I made these cupcakes because they remind me of Romolonia's Marshmallow Meadow.

STRAWBERRY ICED MARSHMALLOW DAISY CAKES

These are sooo easy to make!

Strawberry Iced Marshmallow Daisy Cakes

What you need:
Cake
115g/3¾oz/½ cup softened butter
115g/3¾oz/½ cup caster sugar
115g/3¾oz/1 cup self-raising flour
2 medium eggs, beaten
1 tbsp milk
(makes 12 daisy cakes)

To decorate:
1 packet strawberry fruit smoothie icing (from the supermarket)
or ½ punnet fresh strawberries mixed in a food processor with
200g/7oz/1¾ cups icing sugar
1 packet pink and white marshmallows
small, round pink sweeties

What you do:
Put 12 cupcake cases in a 12-holed cupcake tin. Preheat the oven to 180°C/350°F/gas mark 4.

Put all the cake ingredients into a bowl and use a wooden spoon to mix together. Spoon carefully into the cupcake cases, get a grown-up to help put the tin in the oven, then bake for 18 minutes. Again, get grown-up to help take the tin out of the oven, then leave to cool.

To decorate, make the icing if using fresh strawberries (see above). Spoon a little onto each cake. Using a pair of scissors, cut the marshmallows into halves – you'll need five halves for each cake. Pinch the end of each marshmallow half to form a petal shape. Place five 'petals' in a circle on top of each cake and put a pink sweetie in the middle of each.

Last but not least. For Princess Cornflower,
I've made a flower clock cake!

FLOWER CLOCK CAKE WITH JAM AND CREAM

It's rose
o'clock!

Flower Clock Cake
with Jam and Cream

What you need:
Cake
a little butter to grease the tins
3 medium eggs, beaten
115g/3¾oz/½ cup caster sugar
75g/3oz/¾ cup self-raising flour

To decorate
3 tbsp strawberry jam
small pot double cream, whipped
sifted icing sugar to sprinkle
12 different edible flowers
chocolate ready-to-roll icing

What you do:
Preheat the oven to 200°C/400°F/gas mark 6. Use the butter to well grease two
20.5cm/8 inch sandwich tins (I use silicone cake 'tins' so that my cakes never stick).

Using an electric mixer or whisk, beat the eggs and sugar together for at least 5
minutes. The mixture is ready when it looks like whipped double cream (it seems to
take ages, but don't give up!).

Then, sift the flour through a sieve onto the eggs and sugar and VERY carefully
fold the flour in using a metal spoon. Don't mix or beat hard or all the air will be
knocked out of the cake.

Divide the mixture between the tins, get help to put them in the oven, then bake
for 15 minutes. Get a grown-up to help take the tins out of the oven, then
leave to cool.

When the cakes are cool, tip out of the tins. Spread one cake
with jam and whipped cream, then pop the other cake on
top of it, like a sandwich, and sprinkle the top with
icing sugar.

Place the flowers round the cake and cut clock hands
out of the chocolate icing.

Conversions

Dry Measurements

Metric	Imperial
15g	½ oz
30g	1oz
50g	2oz
90g	3oz
125g	4oz (¼ lb)
150g	5oz
175g	6oz
200g	7oz
225g	8oz (½ lb)

Liquid Measurements

Metric	Imperial	US Cups
30ml	1fl oz	⅛ cup
60ml	2fl oz	¼ cup
90ml	3fl oz	⅜ cup
125ml	4fl oz	½ cup
150ml	5fl oz	⅔ cup
175ml	6fl oz	¾ cup
200ml	7fl oz	⅞ cup
225ml	8fl oz	1 cup
250ml	9fl oz	1 ⅛ cups
300ml	10fl oz	1 ¼ cups
500ml	17 ½ fl oz	2 cups

Here are a few helpful baking tips that
I wanted to share with you...

1. Wash your hands *before you start baking* - fairies don't like germs.
2. Mum says it's healthier to cook with natural ingredients *because they're better for you.*
3. It's a good idea to wear an apron *so you don't get too mucky.* (Billy says he can't *see the point!)*
4. Always ask a grown-up to put things in and take things out of the oven for you.
5. Licking the spoon and bowl is *yummy, but it is dangerous if you have used raw eggs.* If you smile sweetly, you *might be allowed to lick the icing bowl after you* have finished decorating your fairy cakes.
6. If you enjoy cooking, always help to tidy up. My mum gets really cross if I just run off and play *before everything is clean and tidy.* (Washing up can *be quite fun really!)*

Acknowledgements

Team Flossie seems to be growing and I'd like to thank:
Polly, Becca and the team at Anova, Araminta and Philippa from LAW, the brilliant Mary Jones,
Mary Young from Premier Foods, Sarah and Ruth from Renshaw Napier.
Not forgetting Kevin and Mark who have a particular love of fairies!
Special thanks to Carol, Biffy who makes me laugh and last but not least the beautiful Tana!

**McDougalls Flour is highly recommended for all your baking needs.
It makes cakes rise like magic!**

Cherry

If you want to find out more about
Flossie Crums and the fairies
from Romolonia, visit

www.flossiecrums.com

Here you will also find extra recipes and our
online shop for specialist cake decorations.

Crystal